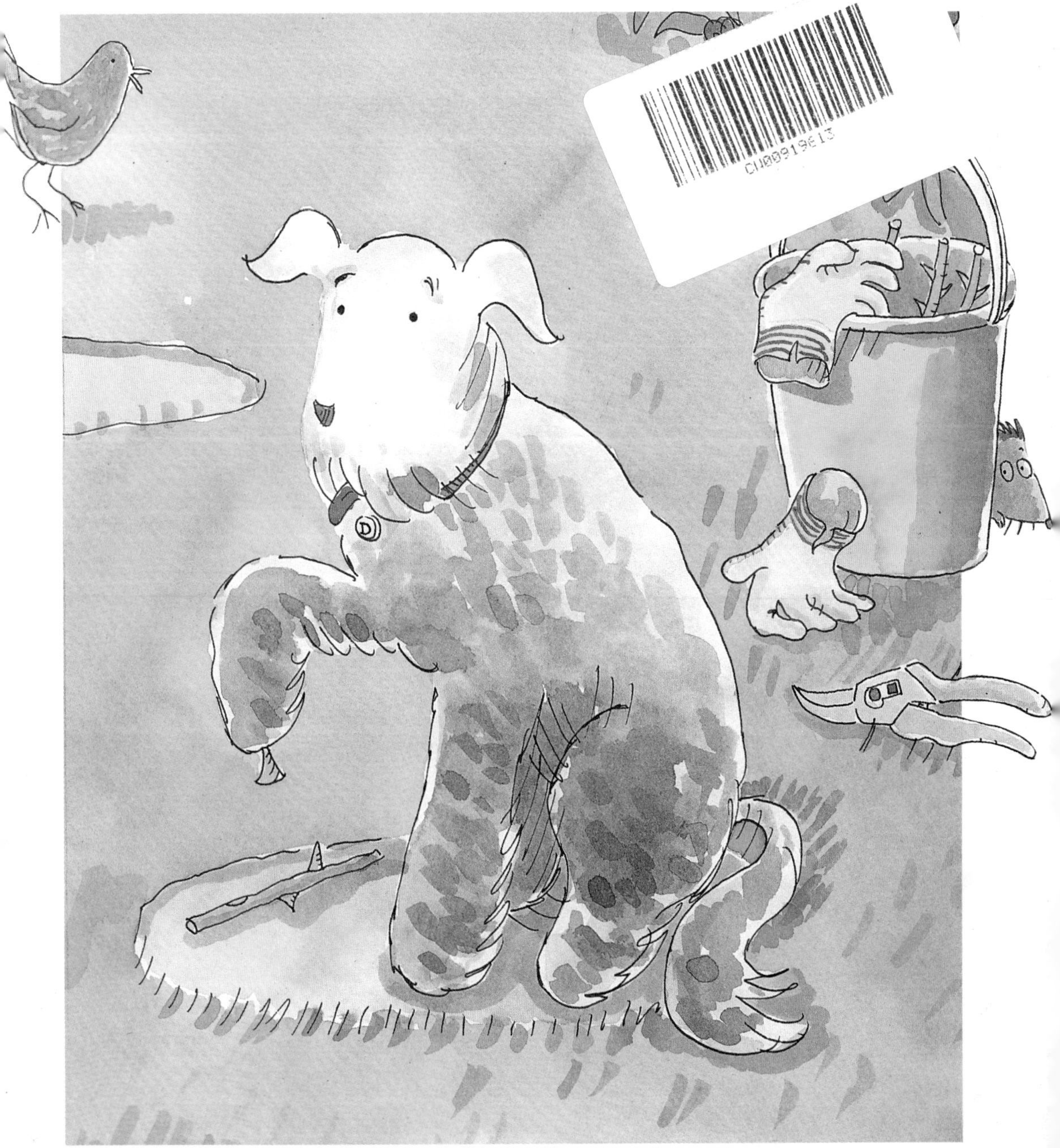

Digger

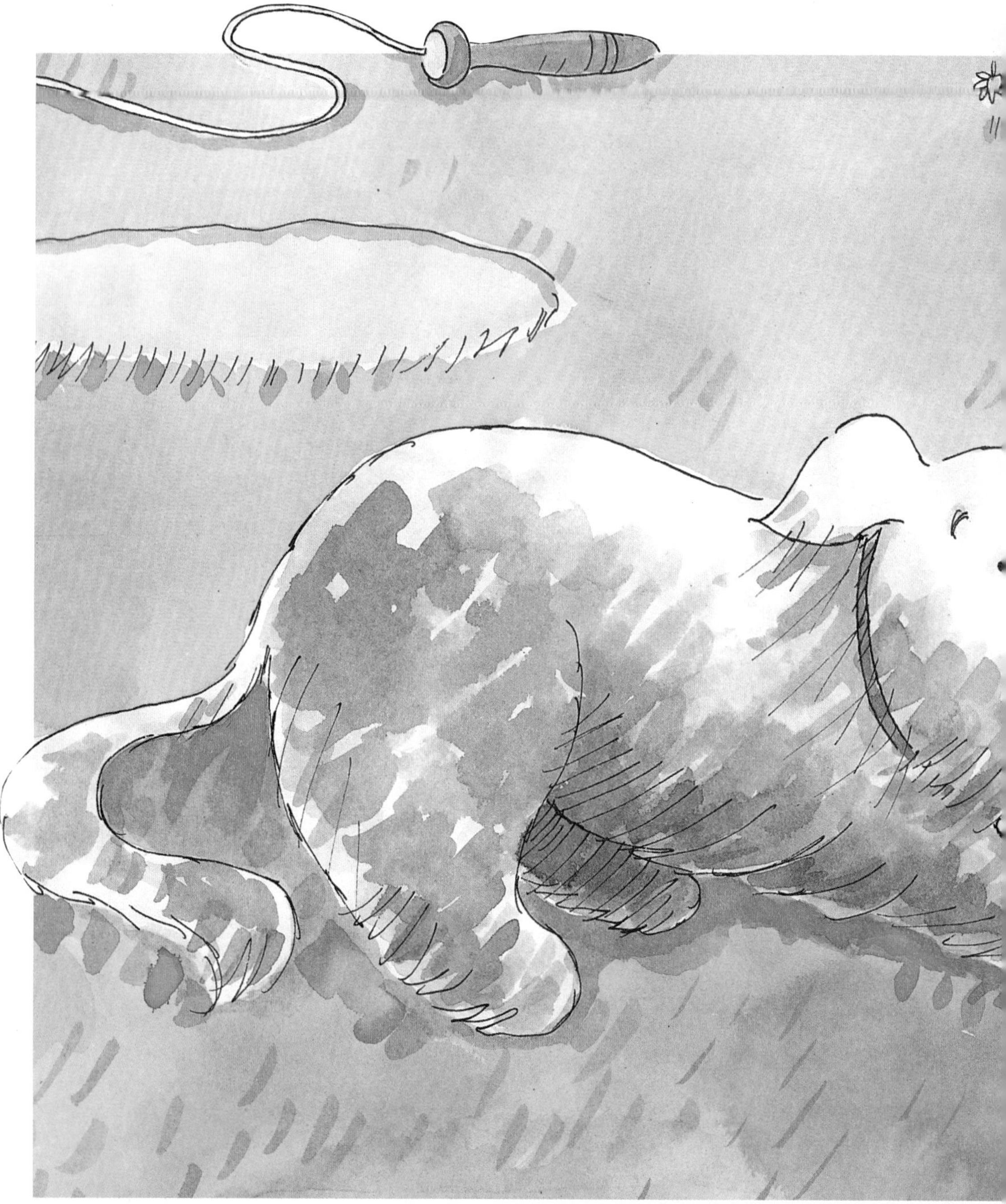

Can you help?

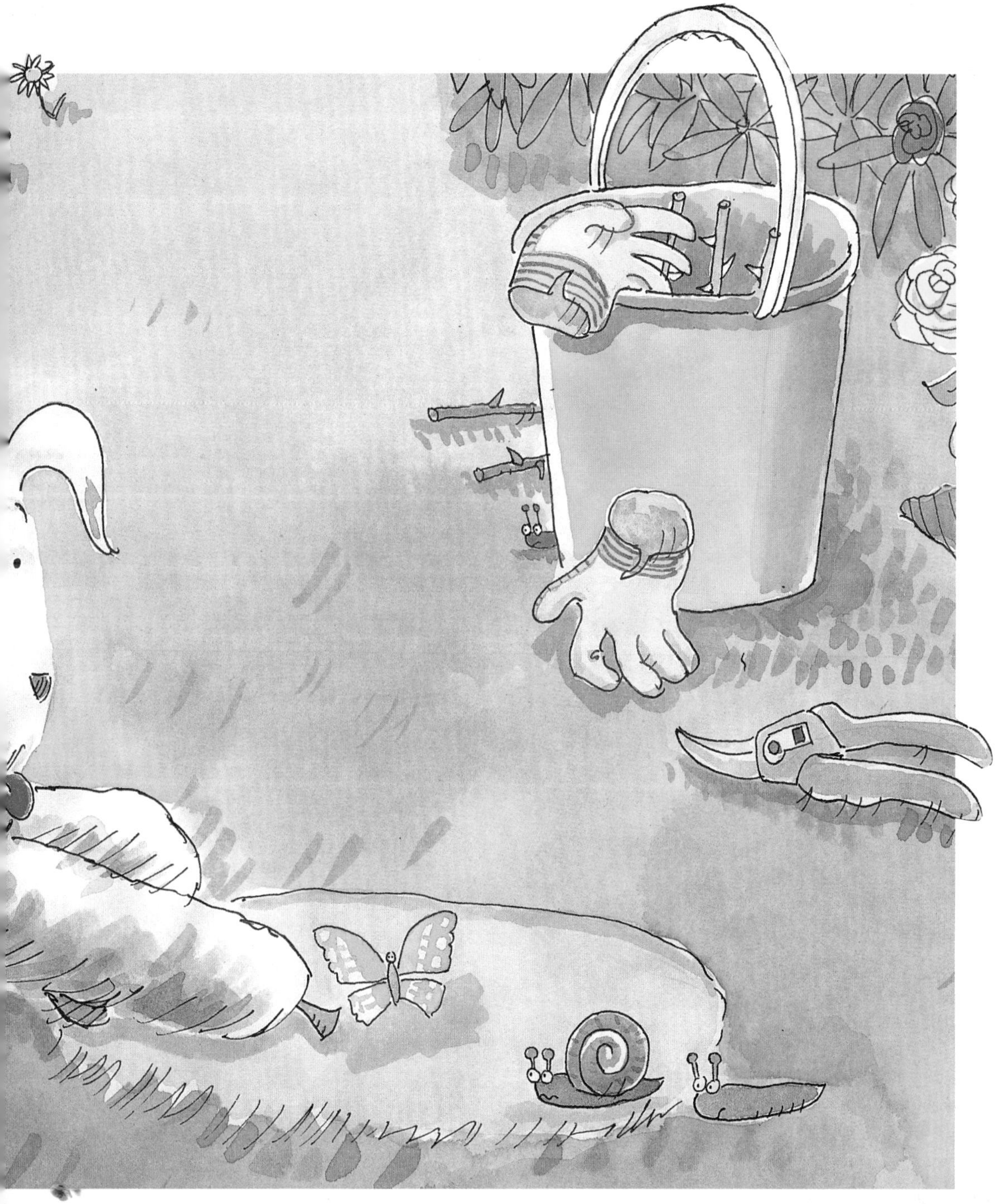

No.

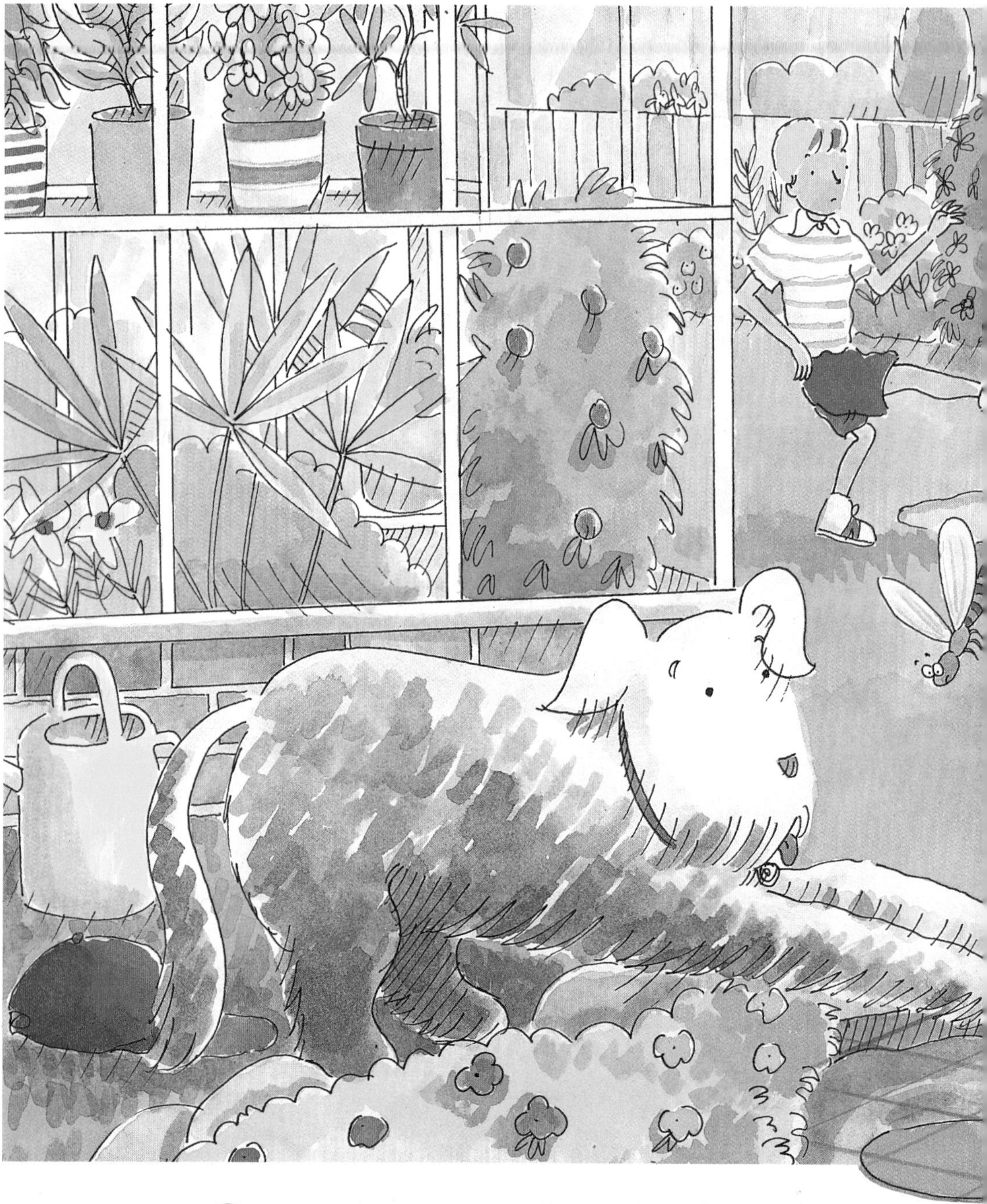

Can you help?

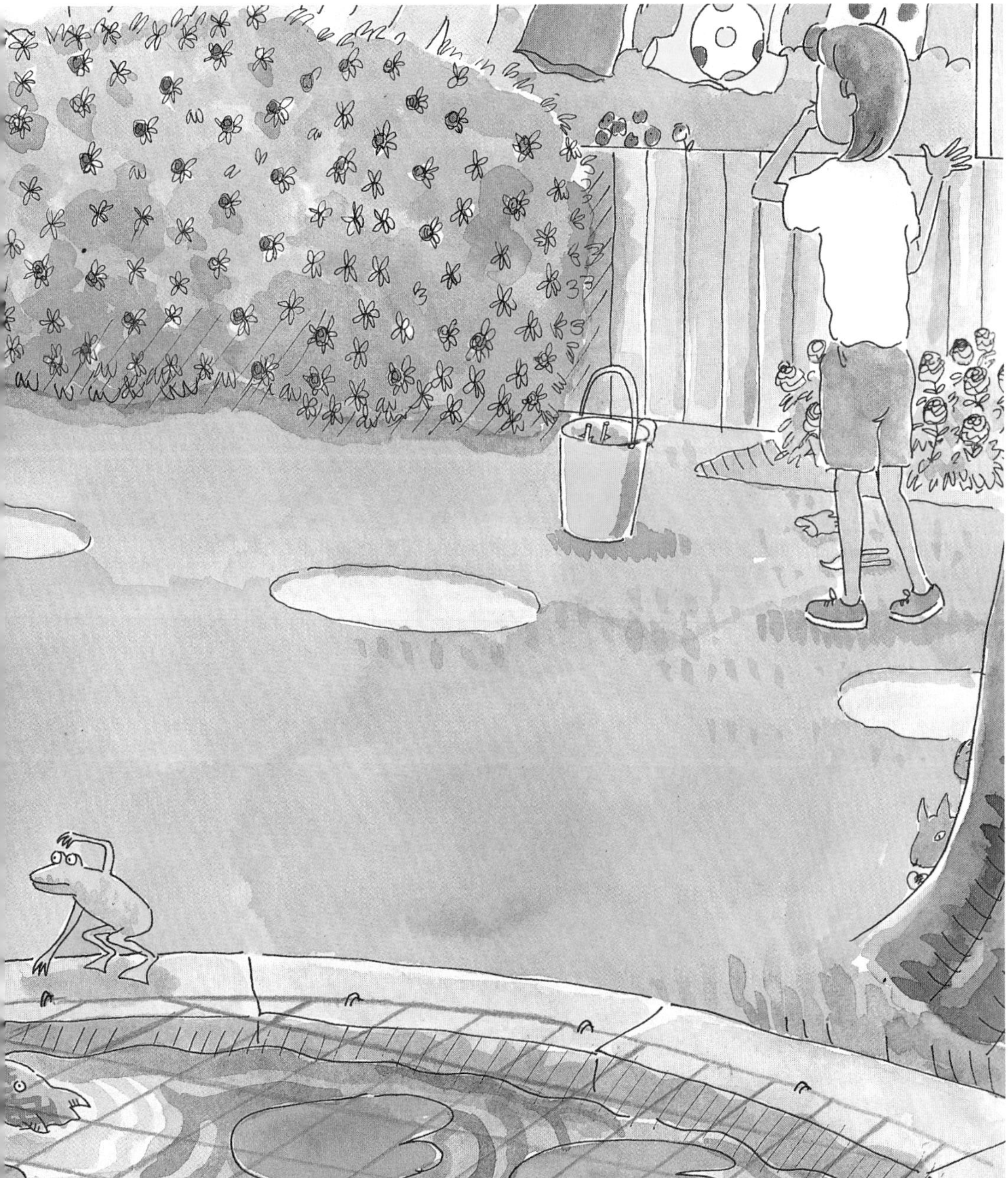

No.

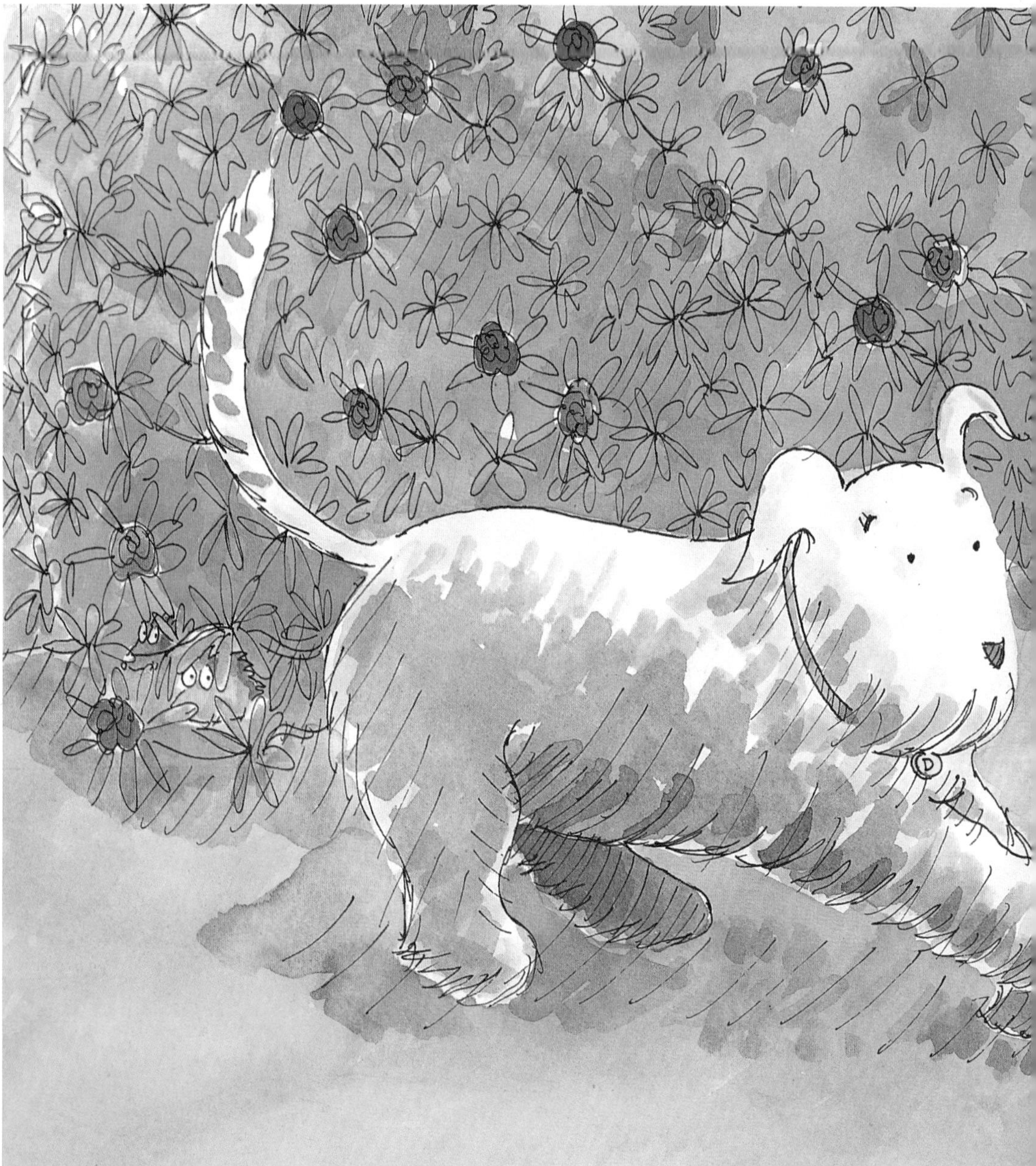

Can you help?

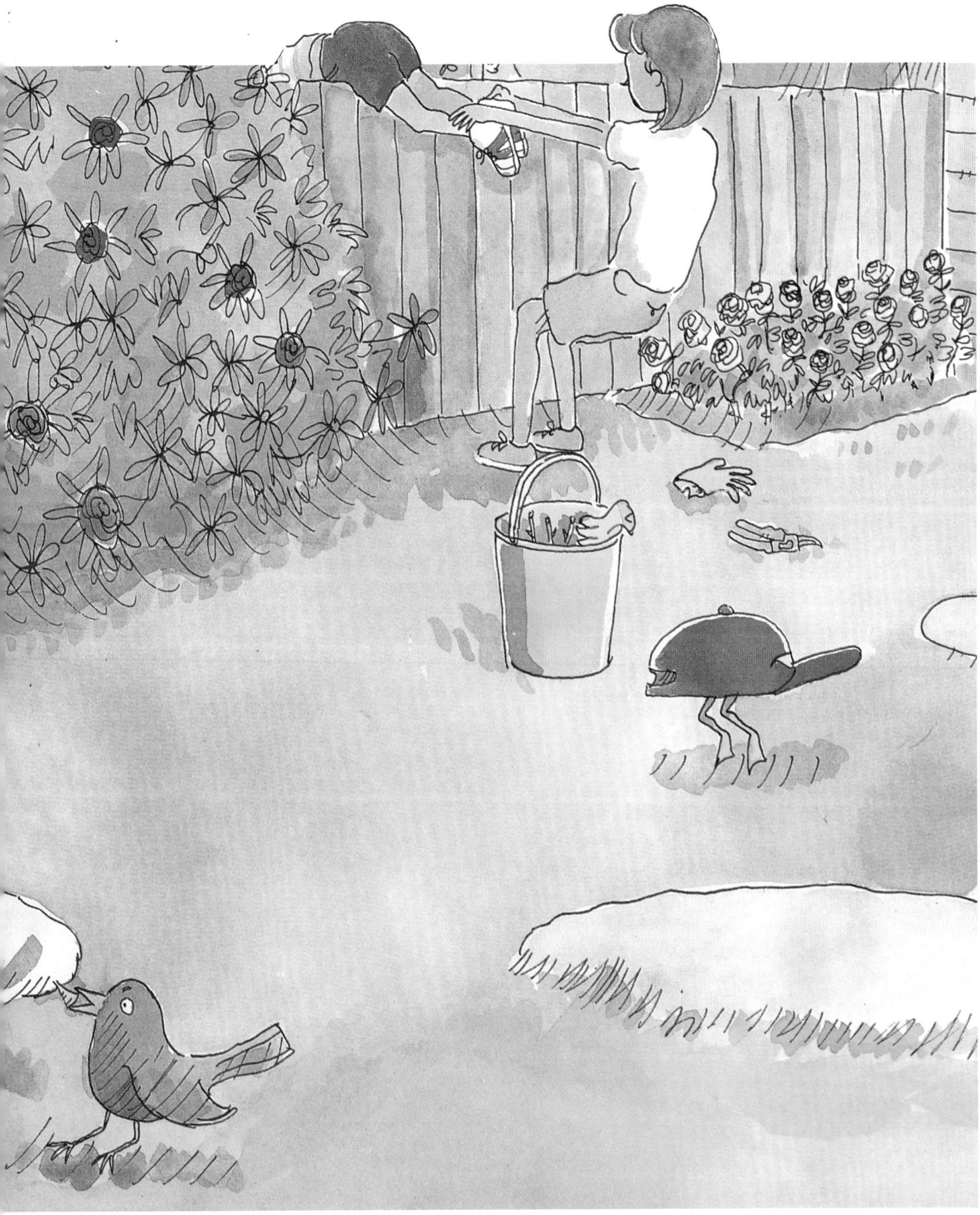

No.

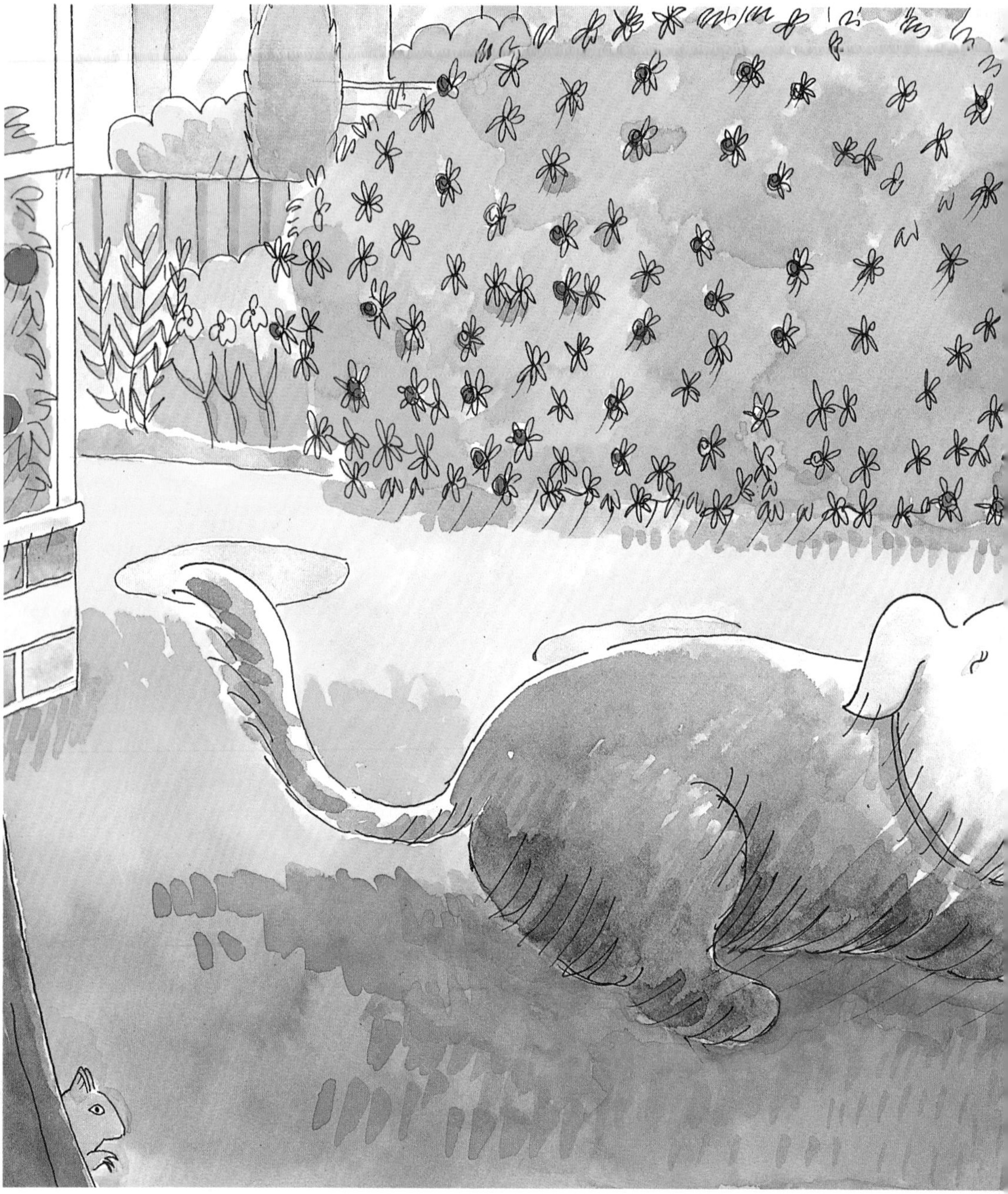

Can you help?

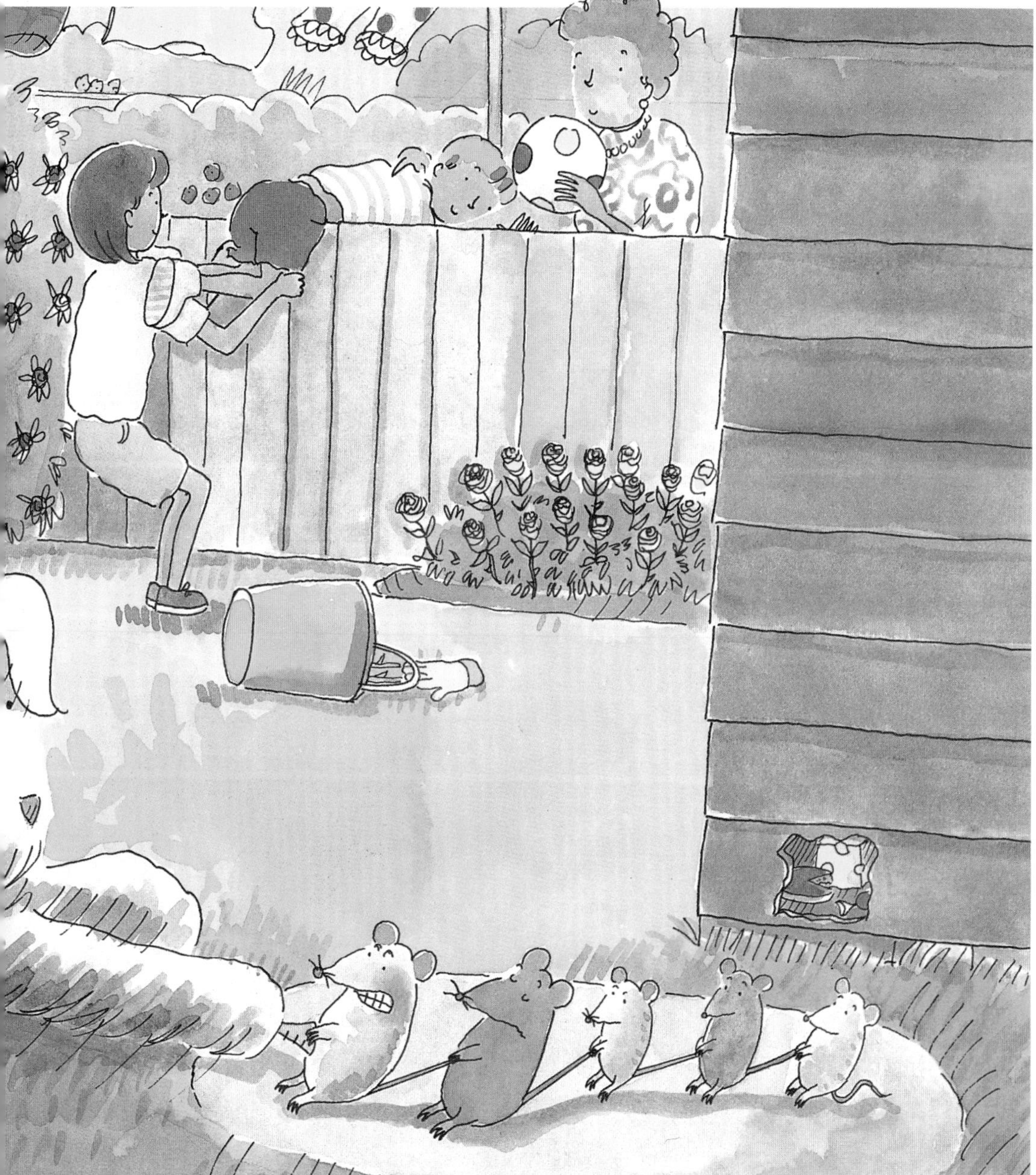

No.

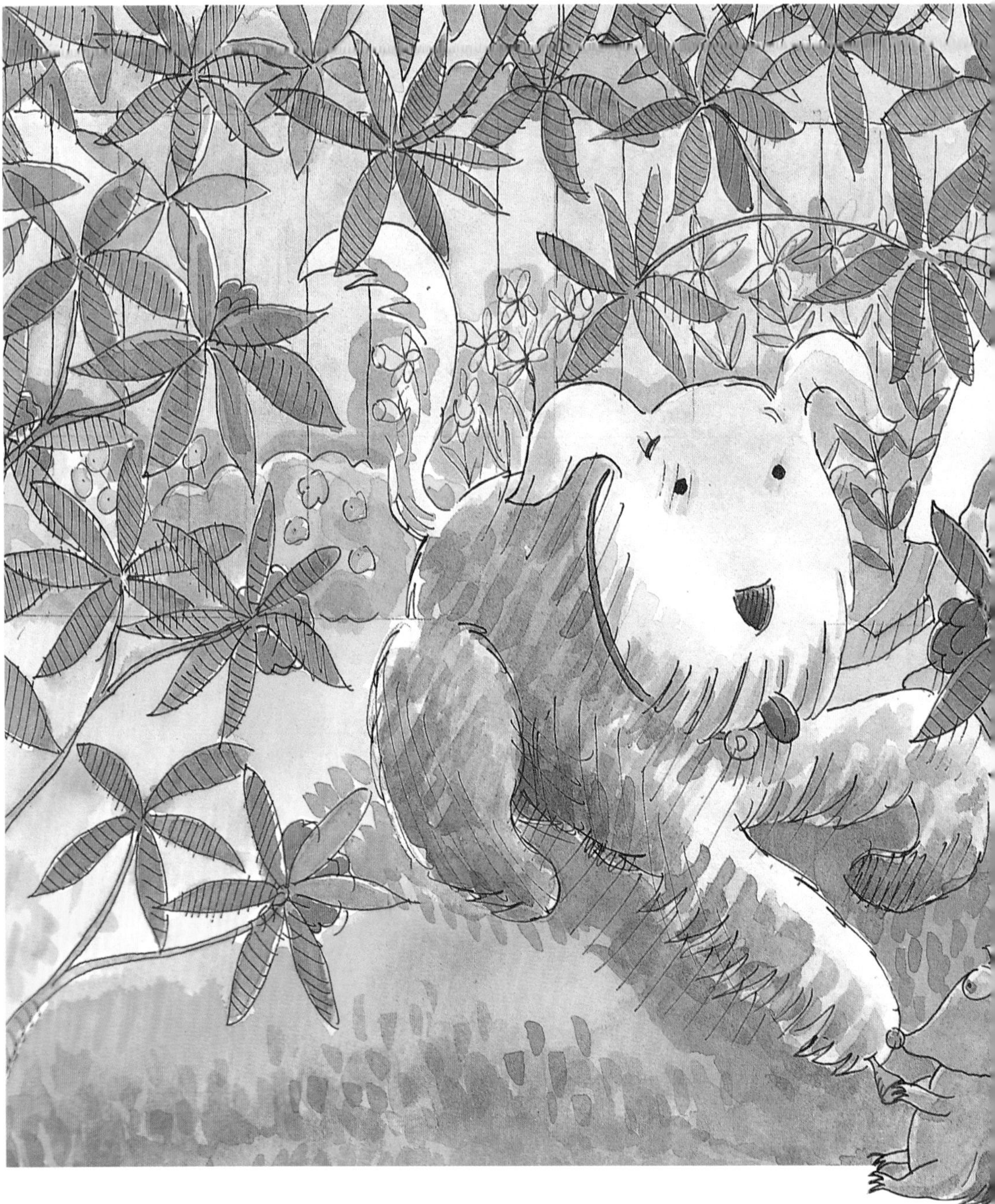

Can you help?

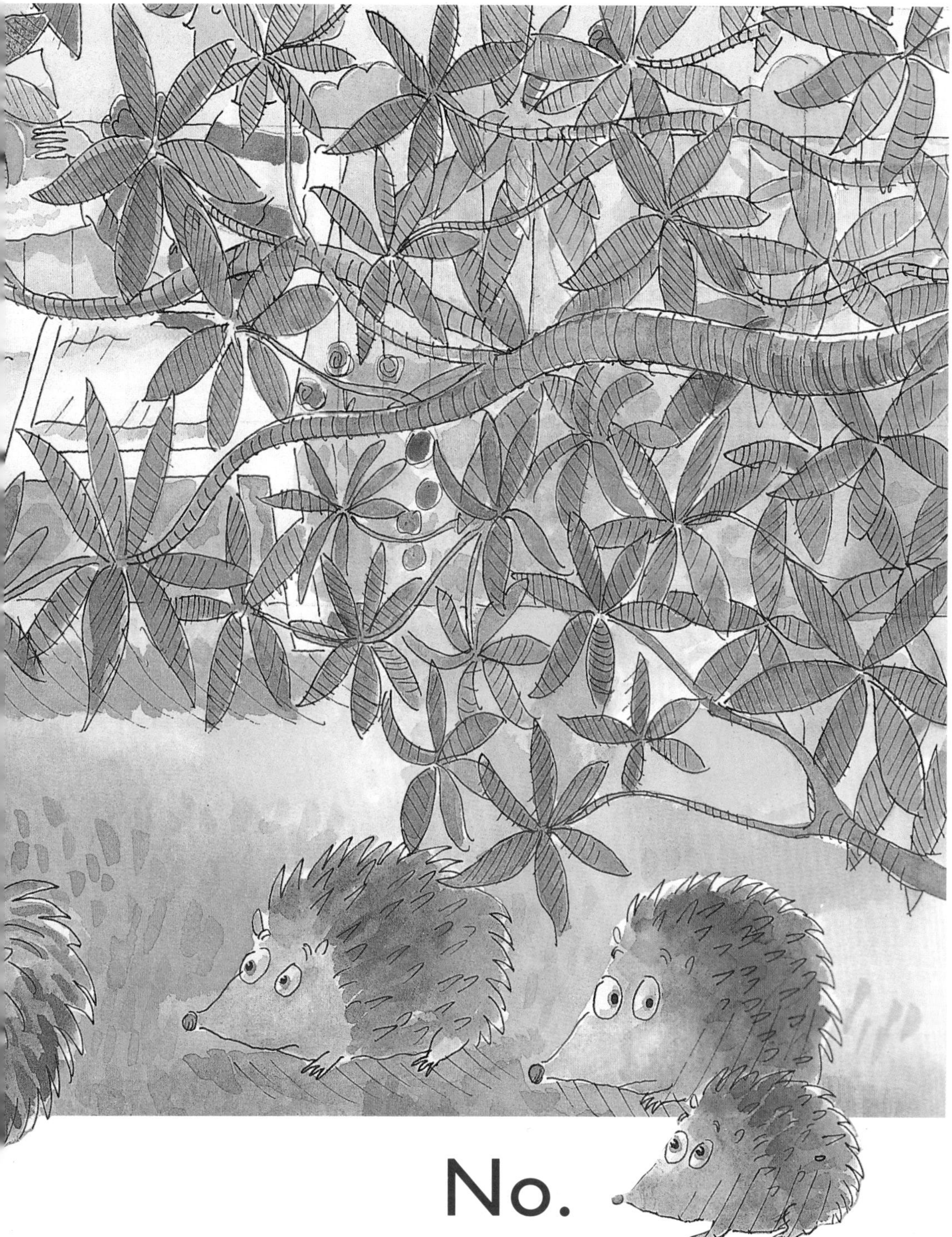

No.

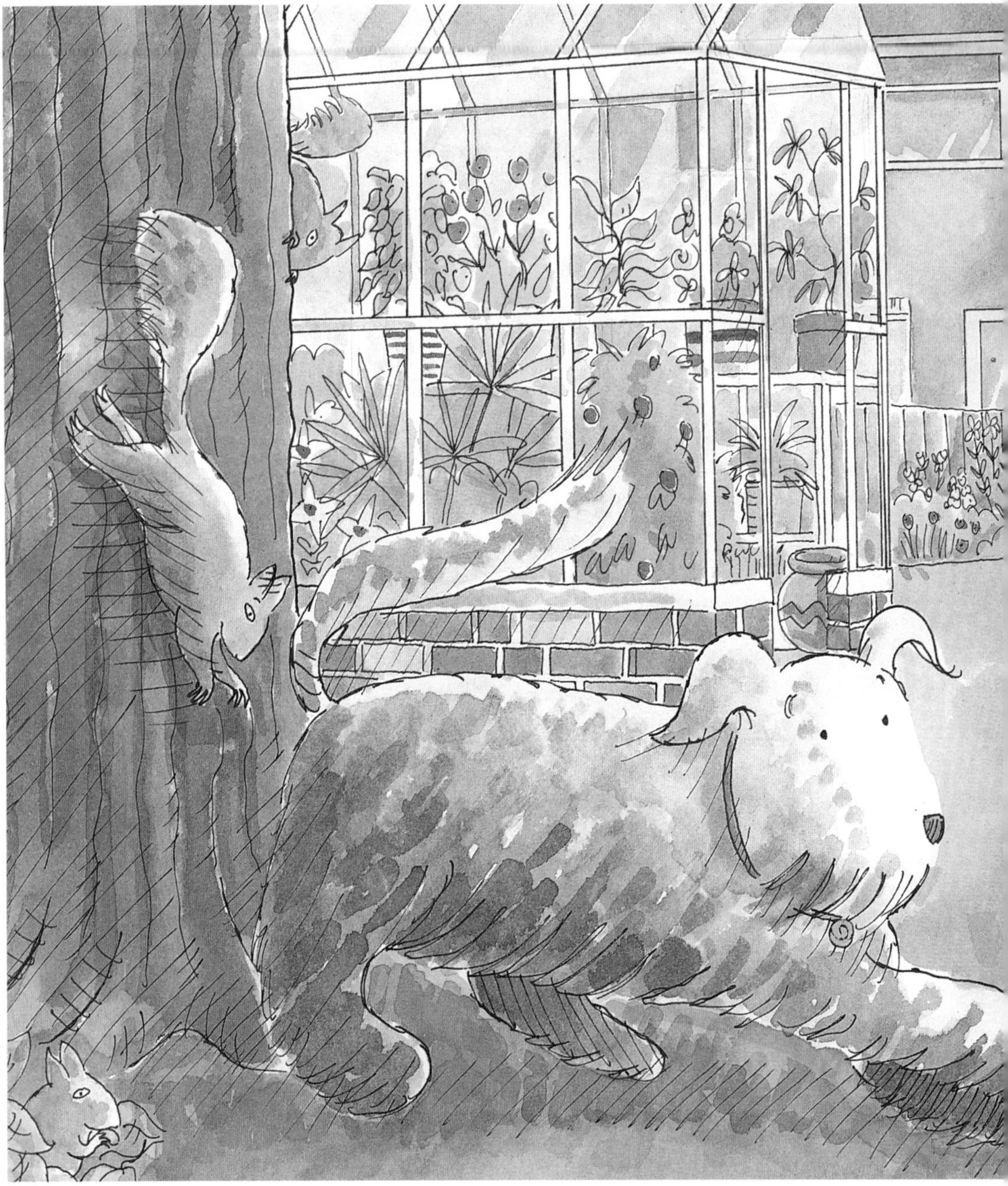

Can you help?

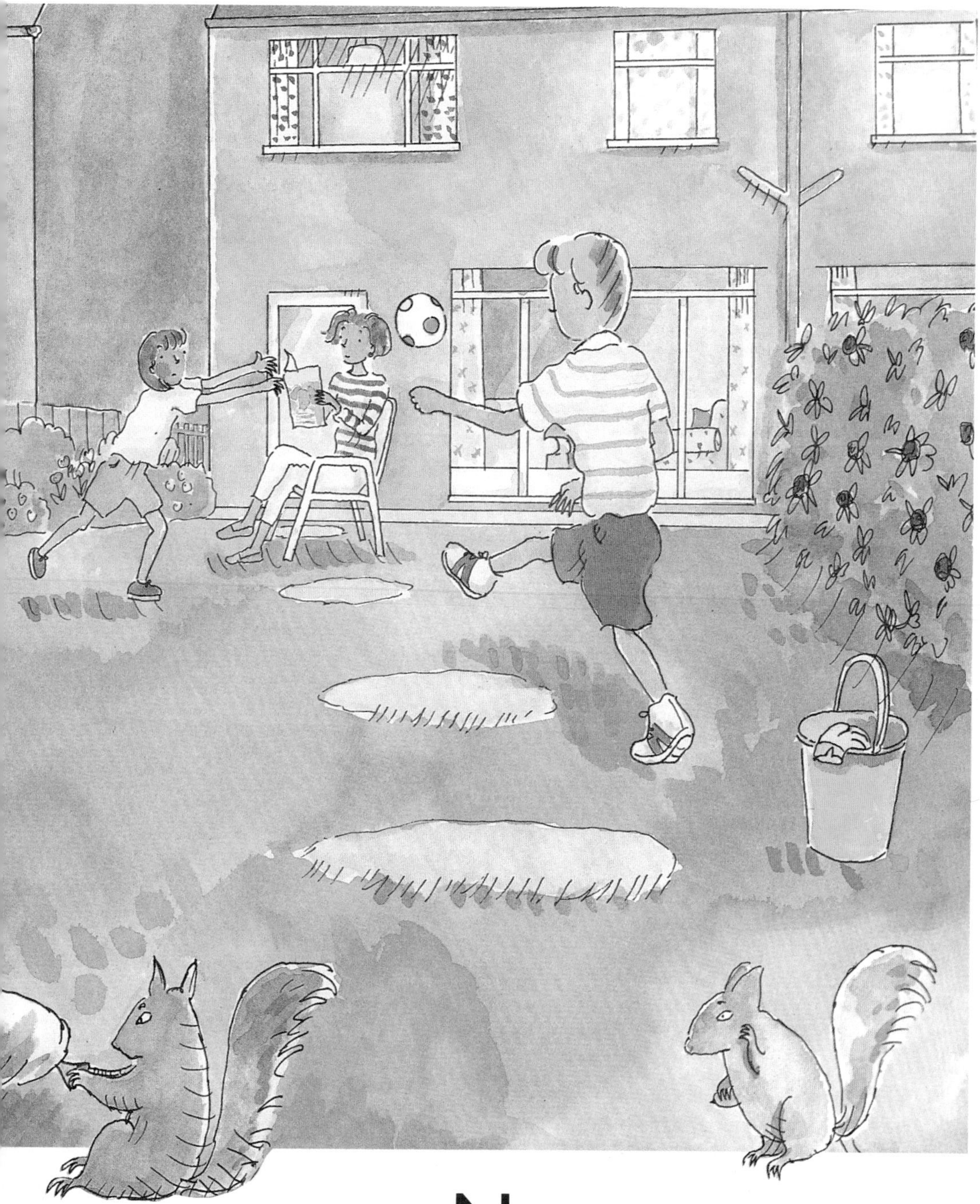

No.

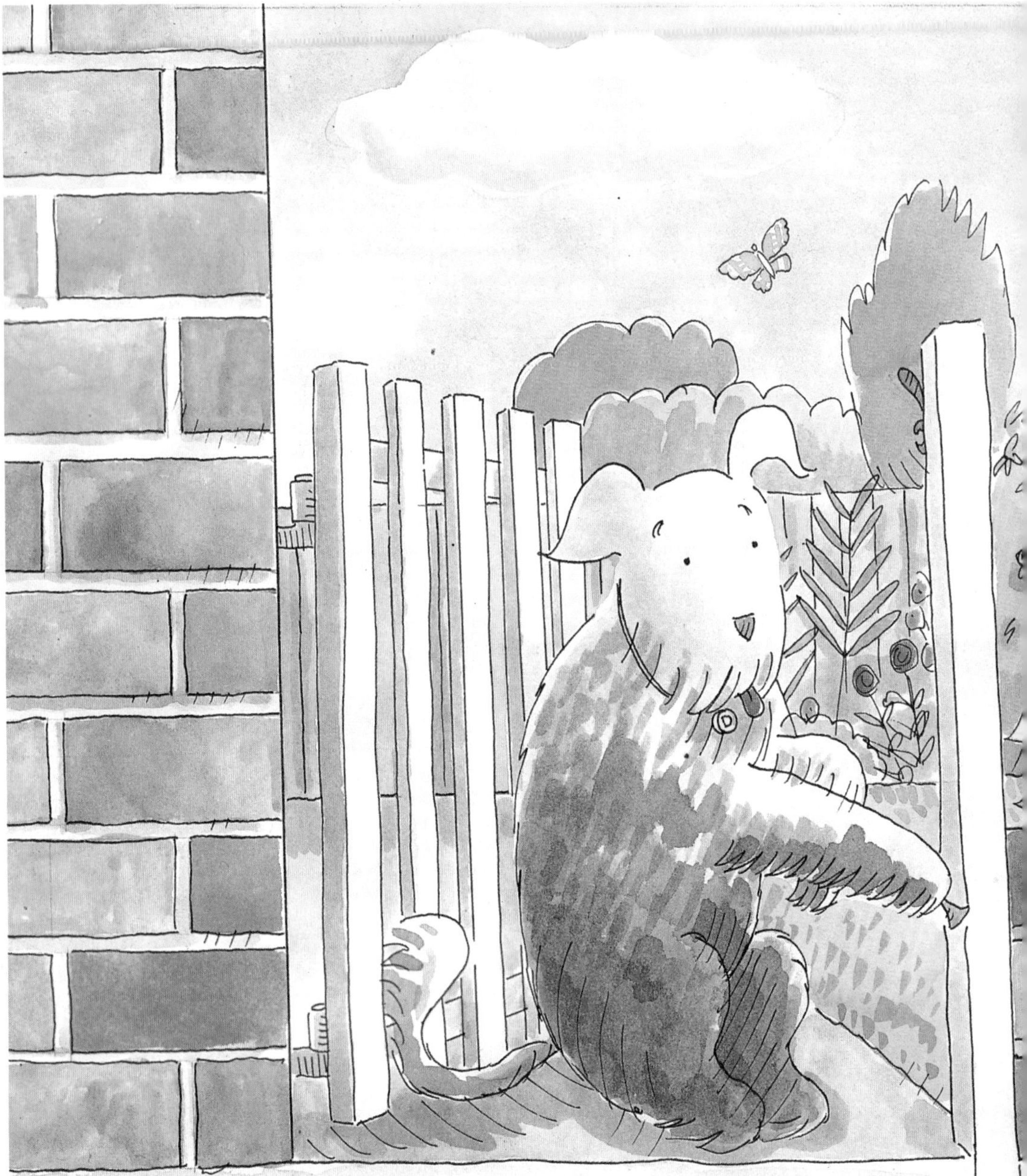

Can you help?

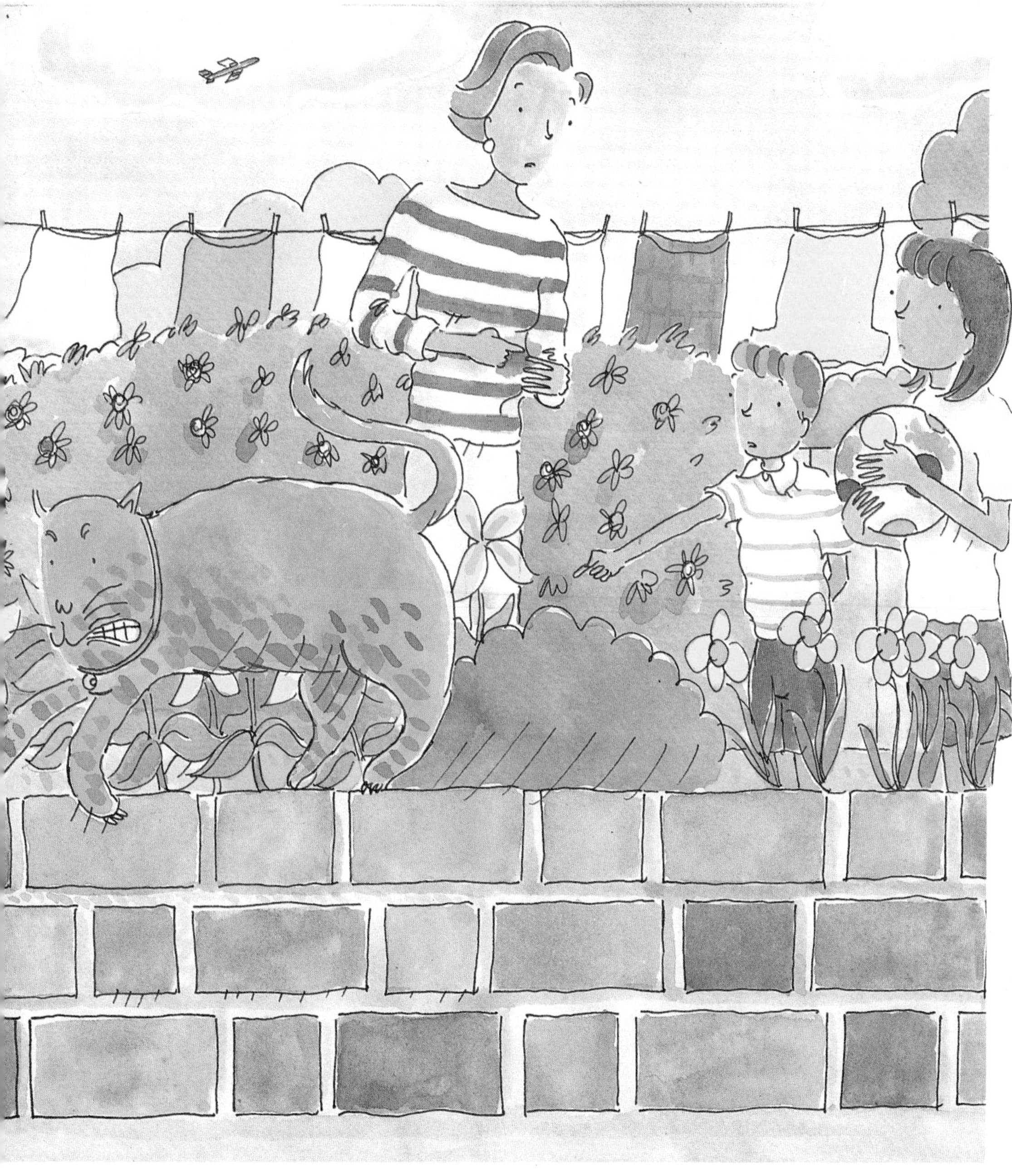

No.

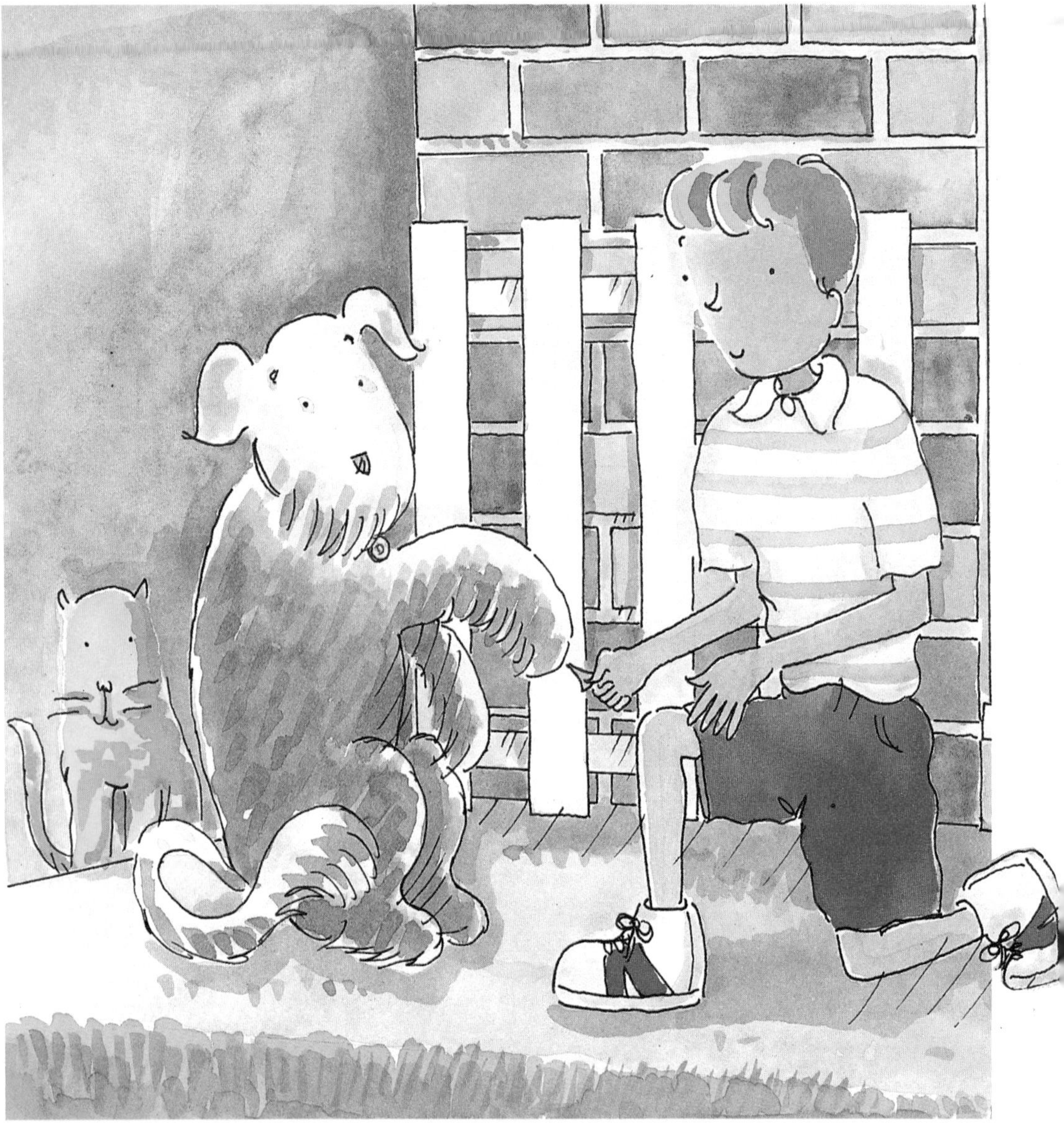

Yes, Digger.
I can help you.